DISNEP
PIRATES of the CARIBBEAN

JACK SPARROW

Dance of the Hours

by Rob Kidd
Illustrated by Jean-Paul Orpinas

Based on the earlier life of the character, Jack Sparrow,
created for the theatrical motion picture,
"Pirates of the Caribbean: The Curse of the Black Pearl"
Screen Story by Ted Elliott & Terry Rossio and Stuart Beattie and Jay Wolpert,
Screenplay by Ted Elliott & Terry Rossio,
and characters created for the theatrical motion pictures
"Pirates of the Caribbean: Dead Man's Chest" and
"Pirates of the Caribbean: At World's End"
written by Ted Elliott & Terry Rossio

DISNEP PRESS

New York

Special thanks to
Elizabeth Braswell, Rich Thomas, and Ken Becker

Dance of the Hours

CHAPTER ONE

"*I* am really *sick* and tired of being *hot* and tired all the time!" Jack Sparrow declared.

He was trudging through the same thick green jungle vegetation he always seemed to be trudging through. Overhead, the yellow sun was as hot as it always was. Trickles of sweat poured down familiar routes on the back of his neck.

"Next adventure, I'm looking for the Northwest Passage," he decided. "Russia and Laplanders. Polar bears and snow and ice.

Miles of ice. Those little cute and furry things, like dogs, what do you call them? You know, all whiskers and big eyes. *Seals! Yes, seals!* Glaciers stretching on forever. Not a single bloody palm tree to be seen."

Despite his protests, things *were* slightly different this time. The palm trees he hated were bent at odd angles, their fronds raised as if frozen midbreeze. The cloud of gnats hovering above the path didn't move in to attack him. In fact, it didn't move at all.

Jack took great, evil pleasure in carefully using his thumb and forefinger to flick each one of the suspended insects out of the air. All went flying into the undergrowth. Except for one, which Jack flicked over his shoulder without looking.

"JACK!"

An equally hot and frustrated Fitzwilliam P. Dalton III cried out in annoyance. He peeled off a flat bug that had hit his forehead, then cleaned himself off with a kerchief.

Of all Jack's latest troubles, the worst was that his entire crew was gone. Except for Fitzy.

It had started out so grandly, Jack reflected. First he had obtained a boat, and then a really grand hat, and a pretty good crew to go with them. It consisted of Arabella, a barkeep's daughter and his first mate, who knew more than a library of books; Tumen and Jean, who were the best sailors you could hope for on a tight ship; plus Constance, who was supposedly Jean's sister, bewitched into the form of a mangy and ill-tempered cat. And there was Tim Hawk, who was young but hardworking and eager to please.

All gone now.

Arabella left to sail with her pirate-queen mother on the *Fleur de la Morte*. Jean,

Tumen, and Constance decided to live out their days on the sunny beaches of the Yucatán. And Tim, who was with them for only a short time, had departed to find out what happened to his family.

Only one crew member was still around.

Fitzwilliam P. Dalton III was, as always, perfectly dressed, from polished buttons to extremely shiny shoes. He looked dapper no matter what rotten hole they were in.

And this annoying situation was *all* Fitzy's fault, really.

After an adventure where the crew had accidentally turned the city of New Orleans bronze . . . and then silver . . . and almost gold . . . they finally managed to restore the city to its normal state and, in the process, found Fitzwilliam's beloved long-lost pocket watch. He said the trinket had been given to him by his sister, who was taken by pirates years ago. It was his only souvenir of her.

It also seemed to be extremely prized by one of the most notorious legends of the Caribbean: the feared captain of the *Flying Dutchman*, Davy Jones.

Jack and Fitzwilliam had barely said good-bye to the rest of the crew of the *Barnacle* and begun their first argument when the tentacle-faced sea captain had appeared on deck, demanding the watch. Things looked mighty grim until Jack began to fiddle with the watch, to see what made it so special—and accidentally stopped time.

Thinking fast, Jack used its time-stopping power to escape Davy Jones. He tied Fitzwilliam to a totem pole—which was really the boat's skiff, reverted to an earlier state—and paddled them both to the closest shore.

Which just happened to be Isla

Esquelética—the island where they had first found Jean and Tumen, and the place where all their adventures began.

The last time they were here, Jack and his crew risked a booby-trapped old temple and the power of the vicious Captain Torrents whose rage would conjure violent storms. And, all the while, they looked for the legendary Sword of Cortés. They wound up stranding Torrents on the island, and the pirate was none too happy about that.*

This time around, Jack and Fitzy had fallen down holes, been captured by human-sacrificing warriors, escaped death from a fiery volcano, and fought off a jaguar. Then they escaped a *strangely familiar* booby-trapped temple housing a very-much-*alive* late pirate, Stone-Eyed Sam with his weird band of European-looking "Aztec" warriors.

* Back in Vol. 1, *The Coming Storm.*

The boys then fled back toward the *Barnacle* . . . and saw Davy Jones's ship anchored in the water right next to the *Barnacle*.

What else was there to do but try stopping time *again* . . . ? And run away.

Land seemed the safest option, since Davy Jones could only set foot on it once every ten years.

The two boys had trudged for hours, past the motionless warriors, beneath the frozen pterosaurs, which the watch seemed to have brought to Jack's era, and through the stock-still jungle.

At least now they had a destination. Ahead lay a port, filled with all sorts of different boats, from all over the world—and from every age.

"Should we not start up time again before going to town? Perhaps some of these sailors can assist us," Fitzwilliam asked, pointing at the motionless ships and the sailors and dockworkers frozen in midtask.

"Good point, Fitzy. Might be a wee bit boring otherwise, too," Jack agreed. Which was a rare thing for him and Fitzwilliam—it had happened only a few times before. Jack looked around. "Just to play it safe, let's get ourselves into that cave over there before we do, though."

Fitzwilliam nodded in agreement.

They clambered up the gray and sandy rocks and squeezed themselves under a narrow overhang. Jack looked around for signs of the jaguar that had attacked him in this same area before, but found nothing.

The two boys settled themselves so that they had a good view of the valley and bay below. They held their breaths. Jack dramatically pressed down on the crown of the watch. It began ticking again.

The rushing sound of the winds of time filled their ears, and once again life snapped to movement.

But things were not as calm and orderly as they had once been. Hundreds of time-trapped pterosaurs now soared overhead, in flocks.

Or is it schools? Jack wondered.

Bands of sailors dressed as Aztecs, hypnotized by the power of the Sword of Cortés and controlled by the pirate Stone-Eyed Sam, who ruled this island, poked through the vegetation, looking for the two boys.

Then things got even stranger.

A dark shadow appeared on the ocean, like a pool of spilled ink. Above it, the sky grew black and stars shone through. The blackness above and shadow below spread rapidly, a cold wind before them. Soon, exactly half the earth and sky were bathed in night. To the east stars twinkled and a bright harvest moon hung in the sky. But to the west was a cloudless Caribbean day, with the sun shining brightly on everything below.

"*There's* something you don't see every day . . . or night . . ." Jack said, swallowing.

Time was turned upside down.

And then, Jack found himself distracted by small rumblings coming from close by.

"Fitzy, can't you control your gastric emissions at a time like this?"

"What . . . ?" Fitzwilliam asked, not really hearing. The scene before him was too absorbing.

There were more rumbles . . . and this time, there was a definite wet and windy sound to them.

"Really, Fitzy! Mind your manners!" Jack cried, holding his nose.

"It is not me, you pompous, poor excuse for a captain!"

The two boys stood up, ready to fight . . . but then there was more rumbling, from *behind* them. They turned to look.

And there stood the feared pirate Captain Torrents, storm clouds gathering around his head.

CHAPTER TWO

*J*ack snapped his fingers.

"Of course. I knew we were forgetting something," he noted, ticking off his fingers. "Dangers of Isla Esquelética are as follows. Stone-Eyed Sam: check. His booby-trapped temple: check. Jungles, heat, vicious insects and animals: check. Captain Torrents, who can summon the power of storms when he's angry—and whom we stranded on said island last time we were here: check. Glad we're all here now."

"I've been waiting myself many a month to find and gut you," the pirate growled.

"There's a bit of a waiting list for that, you know," Jack pointed out.

"Shut yer fool mouth, doomed little man! I'll take my revenge *now*!" Torrents bellowed, reaching for his sword.

Fitzwilliam already had his rapier drawn, and stood at the ready.

"I knew it," Jack sighed. "Pirates have no manners or sense of decency. Always looting and pillaging . . . attacking defenseless ships . . . cutting lines . . ."

With a bloodcurdling scream Torrents leaped at him.

Jack drew his own cutlass. It was rusty and old except for the tip, which was bright, shiny gold.

The pirate captain paused for a moment, surprised by the weird-looking sword.

"Long story, mate," Jack said.*

Then he lunged.

With ugly but accurate skill, Torrents easily deflected the blow.

Fitzwilliam brought his sword quickly up and down, splitting the air with a whistle. But its aim, to distract Torrents, failed completely. The pirate ignored the harmless attack and slashed at Jack.

"Oy, there," Jack said, leaping out of the way. Metal clashed on the rocky cave wall behind him, begetting sparks. Sparks also glowed in Torrents's eyes, previewing the lightning that always came with his anger.

Speaking of which . . . where *was* the lightning? And why was there no indication of a raging storm outside the cave? When Jack's crew stranded him on this island,

* For the full story of how Jack's sword was transformed, be sure to read Vol. 7, *City of Gold*.

Torrents was surrounded by a hurricane that was stirred up by the pirate's anger.

"Hey, Fitzy," Jack called out, swishing his sword in Torrents's general direction. The pirate batted it aside. "Notice anything different since the last time we were here?" Jack asked.

"Besides the pterosaurs, the day becoming night (but only half of it doing so), and dead pirate kings rising from their graves?" Fitzwilliam asked, breathing heavily, as he struck out at Torrents's eyes with his right arm.

"Yes, yes, besides all that," Jack said, waving his hand with dismissive impatience. Without looking, Torrents parried Fitzwilliam and immediately brought his cutlass back up to Jack's belly.

Jack dropped and rolled. "I mean with Captain 'Torn Pants' here. Usually when he's hopping mad there's a storm the size of the Outer Hebrides glowing around his head."

"You are right," Fitzwilliam said, suddenly realizing that they were all dry; no rain, or hail, or even clouds emanating from the cursed sailor. "And he is really quite mad right now."

Captain Torrents laughed evilly, his big, dirty teeth snapping. "I've put my time on this island to good use. Being stranded here made me angry. VERY angry. VERY, VERY ANGRY." With each "very" he brought his sword down, first at Fitzwilliam, then at Jack, then Fitzwilliam again. The boys had to duck to keep their heads. "I don't think this place has ever seen such rain."

"Good for the crops, then, and the soil, too!" Jack said, ducking down low and trying to bring his cutlass up into Torrents's thigh.

But the pirate just kicked him aside, his

boot making a horrible cracking noise against Jack's ribs.

"You all right?" Fitzwilliam called out.

"Oh, aye," Jack wheezed, trying to catch his breath.

The pirate went on, ignoring the conversation. "I realized after a time that I could *control* the curse laid upon me by Davy Jones* . . . harness the energy of storms and bend the elements to my will. If I could control the anger."

"Congratulations, mate, that's lovely," Jack said, picking himself up and raising his sword to protect himself while he recovered. "*More* pirates should learn about anger management."

"Laugh at *this*, why don't you?" Torrents said, grinning. He sheathed his sword,

*As explained to Jack and Fitzwilliam (and the rest of Jack's crew) in Vol. I, *The Coming Storm*.

opened up his hands, and stared at his palms. His big bushy eyebrows knitted together in concentration and his eyes flashed.

Bolts of lightning began to leap from his fingertips—directly at Jack.

"EEEP!" Jack cried, as he daintily hopped out of the way. Smoke rose up from the cave wall behind him. Torrents quickly turned and blew over his hand at Fitzwilliam, like he was puffing away dust. A tiny storm appeared, complete with thunderheads and hail. It flew at Fitzwilliam, blinding him.

Then Torrents turned to the sea and pulled both of his hands into fists.

On cue, two giant waterspouts rose up from the waves

As Torrents pulled his hands toward his chest, the spouts bent and raced up the hillside toward the cave, destroying every-thing in their path.

"I would be worried," Jack said as calmly as he could in the face of doom, "if we didn't have a little supernatural what-have-you of our own."

With a triumphant sneer, Jack whipped out the watch. Very dramatically, he pulled the crown to stop time.

But nothing happened.

Jack tried again.

And again nothing.

He shook the watch, then noticed its face: the minute and hour hands were going crazy, spiraling in different directions around and around the face.

"What now, Jack?" Fitzwilliam asked.

"Well, Fitzy-me-mate, I think it's time for good ol' Plan B," Jack said, delicately closing the watch and pocketing it.

"We run," Fitzwilliam sighed tiredly.

"We run," Jack agreed.

Both turned to go.

But Torrents threw open his fists and the waterspouts he had summoned grew huge, blocking the entrance of the cave. Jack and Fitzwilliam could see down to the belly of the vortexes: swirling, gray doom.

"Good-bye, lads," Torrents laughed, pulling the waterspouts hand over hand like he was hauling up a water bucket. "I've got just the right island retreat for you to spend the rest of your days. Aw, who am I kidding—you only have *minutes* left to live. Anchors aweigh!"

The two waterspouts opened up and sucked in Fitzwilliam and Jack.

Around them, water and twigs and stones—and the occasional surprised small animal—whirled viciously. The boys watched the blurry world disappear below them as they were carried high into the air.

They passed over the hypnotized sailor-warriors and through a flock of pterosaurs that fell screaming out of the way.

They passed from the sunny side of the island to the dark, and up into the mountains.

A sulfurous-smelling cloud rose up.

"Blast it, Fitzwilliam, can you not control your bowels like a man when the going gets rough?" Jack demanded.

"I told you before, I will tell you again. It is not me," Fitzwilliam called back from inside his own waterspout. He sounded less angry than nervous.

And for good reason. Below them rose up the angry, jagged cone of the goddess Chantico's volcano.*

The waterspouts dipped. It was obvious where they were going to drop the two boys.

* Jack and Fitzwilliam were nearly killed there in Vol. 8, *The Timekeeper.*

A mighty rumbling—far greater than Torrents's small storms—issued up from the volcano. The ground below them began to shake. Spurts of acrid, black smoke issued forth like an angry teakettle. Red-gold lava began to bubble out through the volcano's cracks.

The waterspouts dipped more, and Jack and Fitzwilliam were spat out on a narrow lip of the volcano, just below the top. They were too bruised and banged up from the ride to move much. But it didn't matter: the sheer height of the walls above and below them meant escape would be impossible.

The volcano shuddered and rumbled again. The two boys stumbled, desperate not to fall off. An explosion of lava shot into the air.

"Escaping a volcanic eruption once, maybe. Doing it twice. . . ? Methinks we're dead dock meat, mate," Jack said sadly.

CHAPTER THREE

*J*ack gritted his teeth and took a deep breath, bravely preparing for the end. Fitzwilliam was probably doing the same. Jack couldn't be sure; his own eyes were tightly shut. All he knew was that *he* wasn't going to scream first.

For the first time he was *glad* Arabella, Jean, Tumen, Constance, and Tim weren't with them.

"Well, maybe Constance," Jack couldn't help muttering. "I wouldn't mind seeing her go first, mangy cat."

"What was that you said?" Fitzwilliam asked.

"Nothing—just choosing last words."

"Oh. Right," Fitzwilliam said.

Their banter was cut short by the wall of heat that hit them. It came from below, blasting their whole bodies. It burned from their faces to their sweaty toes.

"Good-bye, Jack Sparrow. It has been . . . most interesting," Fitzwilliam yelled out.

"That's *Captain* Jack Sparrow," Jack yelled back.

Flames began to lick at their fingers, little tickles of feathery heat. The soles of their shoes and boots began to slip into the ground as the rock itself melted.

Jack prepared himself for searing, burning pain . . .

. . . but it actually felt pretty good.

He had been in a Navajo sweat lodge once

(long story, mate) and it felt a lot like this. Beads of perspiration broke out on his brow, but it felt cleansing, not deadly. And the waves of heat were doing wonders for his back. All of those hours of standing up and steering the ship melting away like magic . . .

Jack cracked open an eye.

Yes, they were at the edge of a fiery, doomy pit. Yes, they were standing on a small rocky archipelago above a sea of red-hot lava. Yes, there was magma and sparks and embers and ash swirling through the air in an apocalyptic maelstrom.

But not a hair on his head had been singed. And there was no smell of burning flesh. Only that awful sulfur stink.

He looked over at Fitzwilliam. The nobleman's son was poised heroically: chest out, jaw set, standing firm, prepared to die.

But still very much alive.

"Too bad," Jack grumbled. Then he cupped his hands around his mouth and shouted: "Open your eyes, mate. You're not dead."

Fitzwilliam did as he was told, blinking into the bright light.

Sheets of flame rose up and passed over them . . . without leaving a mark. Just that feeling of healing warmth.

Fitzwilliam passed his hand through a flame in wonder.

The fire started changing colors, as if it were growing hotter. Tips of yellow and orange flames began to glow white and then blue, burning at temperatures the two boys could only imagine—since they didn't actually *feel* any hotter.

The flames danced faster, and closer together. Then they merged into one thick blazing column. The inferno shifted and changed shape: hands and arms separated out of the brightness, and then a head formed out of the heat. A woman made of pure white fire stepped forward.

Fitzwilliam and Jack watched, dumb-struck.

The flames died down and her features became clearer: high cheekbones and a sharp nose. Ash and ringlets of smoke swept back over her ears like hair. Her eyes were flame-blue with no pupils. Her face was perfectly smooth, with lips that looked like they were carved from stone.

"I am Chantico, goddess of the volcano and protector of this island." Her voice sounded like it came from everywhere at once. It completely lacked expression or emotion.

"Pretty cold demeanor for a goddess of fire," Jack couldn't help observing out loud.

"*That* is how you address a *goddess*?" Fitzwilliam whispered angrily.

"Pardon if I am not familiar with the etiquette," Jack answered back, shrugging. "This is the first goddess I've met."

"*You* are the ones who have meddled with the proper flow of time," she accused them. Her fine eyebrows gathered slightly. "The hours are dancing again, and it is *your* fault!"

Jack gulped. Chantico might have appeared cold, but it was obvious she was capable of annoyance. Maybe even rage. Something he did not want to personally witness.

He tried to stealthily reach into his pocket and tuck the watch further in. After all, she didn't have any *proof* that they were the ones responsible . . .

"OUCH!" he yelped.

The watch had turned white-hot in his

hand. He instinctually dropped it and stuck his fingers in his mouth.

"No!" Fitzwilliam cried as the watch started to bounce over the lip, into the volcano itself.

But one of the tongues of white flame caught it, and held it in the air.

"Another tool of man," Chantico said with disgust, looking at the watch. "Interfering with the ways of nature."

"Aye, bad men and their watches, foul beasts," Jack agreed, still sucking on his burned fingers. "You should see our compasses and harpsichords. Pure devilry!"

"This island has seen many lives," the goddess sighed, ignoring him. She turned from the watch and looked out beyond the volcano. "Many histories. Many people have come and gone. They breed and build their edifices upon the land . . . which are eventually washed away into the sea, as all things are with time."

"What's an '*eddy-fiss*'?" Jack whispered to Fitzwilliam.

"A building, you idiot," Fitzwilliam shot back.

It was a far more disappointing definition than Jack had hoped.

"*With* his . . . *buildings*, and his toys, man always tries to stop the natural order of things. I had thought we would be free from it for a time. The mad king with his ridiculous little sword who ruled a city that should never have been . . ."*

Chantico shook her head. "He was finally stripped of power, and the natural order returned."

"Ridiculous little sword?" Fitzwilliam

* Chantico is referring to Stone-Eyed Sam, whose story is told in Vol. i, *The Coming Storm*.

whispered. "She cannot mean the Sword of Cortés!"

Jack grinned proudly and spoke up thinking about the magical, powerful sword. "We were there! In the time of the mad king. Awful mess. Of course, we were there after, too, when he was dead. Which was actually the first time we came to this island. *Before* he was alive. Again. If you catch my meaning."

Chantico raised one fiery brow at him. She could have been angry or amused. There was no way to tell.

"Behold your dangerous toy," she said, indicating the watch with one long, flamy finger.

Jack and Fitzwilliam turned to look. The watch's hands had stopped spinning! The two boys looked up at the sky eagerly. But even through the ash and flame they could see it was still split in two: night and day.

And as if just to prove the point, another flock of pterosaurs screamed overhead. Nothing was back to normal.

"Look again," Chantico ordered.

The two boys looked back at the watch. Slowly, almost reluctantly, the minute and hour hands drew back until they were both lined up at 12 on its face.

"You have twelve hours to repair the damage you have done," said the goddess. Tendrils of blue flame rose from her hair and fingers. She was about to be absorbed back into the flames that surrounded her. "If the island has not returned to its natural course when the clock again reads twelve, I will destroy you and find one who *can* stop the dancing of the hours."

Her eyes burned—literally. She fixed them on Jack.

"Oh, well, *thank* you, your goddess-ness,"

Jack said sarcastically, bowing. "We're *so grateful* to be given this chance to fix things before you destroy us and find someone better. Do you know what that sort of talk does to a lad's self-esteem? You automatically assume there's a chance we're going to muck it up, and are already lining up some sort of *better* adventurer who can . . ."

Chantico opened her mouth wide, so wide it was as though her head had split open. They could see past her tongue all the way down her throat.

"Ah," Jack cleared his own throat, nervous that he might have actually overdone it this time.

Chantico let out a mighty roar. It sounded like it came from the depths of the volcano itself. With it came a hot wind and swirls of ashes that surrounded the two boys.

Jack screamed; the soot pouring out of

Chantico's mouth burned his eyes, and the sparks singed his face. Fitzwilliam swore profusely, using words Jack had never heard him use before.

Finally the wind died down and the flames petered out around their feet. The ashes settled into little black piles.

Fitzwilliam's pocket watch rocked on its perch of thin air. Then it fell, landing on one of the piles of ash.

The boys were no longer on the lip of the volcano but on its north side, looking down at the port with the ships from ages gone by.

Jack picked up the watch. He blew on it, raising a little cloud of soot. He used his shirtsleeve to polish the dial, and saw that the hands had started moving normally again.

He groaned. They had already lost a minute.

CHAPTER FOUR

$\mathcal{T}$welve hours was not much time to, well, reorder time for a whole island (or perhaps it was the entire world that was affected; Jack didn't really know). He didn't even know where to begin looking for help. Jack uneasily eyed the port in the distance—it would take at least six hours to get down there from where they were. Add in slogging-through-the-jungle time and asking around just to *maybe* find someone who knew how to "stop the hours dancing . . ." It was going to be tight at best.

Fitzwilliam was obviously thinking the same thing.

"I suppose we had better find a way down," he said, walking over to the edge of the path where they stood. He bent over to get a better look, hoisting his noble derriere in the air.

"Steady there," Jack muttered as he fought the urge to give his companion a kick in the royal rear. It would be so funny . . . and deserved!

Apparently, he wasn't the only one who noticed Fitzwilliam's vulnerable position. A pterosaur swooped down out of the sky, its foot claws open and extended to grab the aristocrat.

In a second Jack had his sword out.

He leaped between Fitzwilliam and the prehistoric beast. Claws clanged against the sword's rusty old metal. The pterosaur screamed and fell sideways, spiraling down the outside of the volcano.

Fitzwilliam jumped back, unharmed.

"Best be careful there, Fitzy," Jack said, indicating the boy's hind side with his sword. "Apparently these Uglybirds think you would make a tasty snack. That one was almost big enough to carry you away."

Fitzwilliam paled and stood back from the edge. "My thanks, Jack. I did not even see . . ."

But Jack was already thinking about something else. *Almost big enough to carry you away.* He frowned and looked up at the sky. Different-size pterosaurs circled and wheeled on the hot currents above the volcano. There were golden orange ones, and bluish green ones, and ones with what looked like sort-of-feathers growing off their shoulders. And even some that were absolutely massive, like Chinese kites.

Kites.

Jack started jumping up and down and waving his arms like a lunatic.

"Uglybird food! Come and get it! Dinner bell's rung, you flying scalawags! Tasty human here! Get a look at this!" He pulled up his shirt and showed his belly. (Which was, truth be told, a bit scrawny.) "Looks good, don't it? MMMMM!"

"Jack!" Fitzwilliam called in horror.

Jack ignored him. A small pterosaur swooped down, aiming at his eyes.

"Off with you, you minnow among whales!" Jack shouted, knocking the thing aside with his hands. "It's the *big ones* I want!"

"What in the name of deuce are you doing, Jack? Has the heat from the volcano driven you mad?"

Finally a large pterosaur turned its golden eyes toward Jack and dove. The captain of the *Barnacle* waited until the absolute last minute, gauging the beast's razor-sharp claws.

Then Jack jumped up, in an attempt to grab them.

Confused, the pterosaur wheeled away. It was not used to dinner trying to feed *itself* to him.

"You *are* mad," Fitzwilliam said softly.

"I'm trying to hitch a ride, mate, and I seriously suggest you do the same . . . unless you want to waste your time around here waiting for ol' Fire-Breath to come back and destroy you."

Fitzwilliam blinked, staggered by the genius and simplicity of the plan. "That's bloody brilliant, Jack."

He drew his sword, which shone and

flashed in the sun residing in the portion of the sky that was still day-lit. "This might help a bit—Father was a bit of a birder. He said that some birds of prey *love* shiny objects."

"A useful fact-let. Thanks to you, Fitzwilliam's dad," Jack said.

The pterosaurs grew agitated and circled faster. It wasn't long before a large one swooped down at Fitzwilliam.

With all of its attention focused on the shiny sword, Jack had no trouble leaping up and grabbing on to its knobby claws.

Surprised by the sudden extra weight, the beast lunged to the side, *away* from Fitzwilliam.

"Grab on!" Jack yelled.

Fitzwilliam put the hilt of his sword in his teeth and leaped. He had no trouble getting a hold of Jack's legs and hung from his ankles.

The pterosaur, however, was having a tougher time.

It wobbled from side to side for a moment, trying to keep gliding with the two boys hanging from its feet.

But the weight was too much. It finally just folded its wings and collapsed to the ledge. Fitzwilliam and Jack rolled away, unhurt but disappointed. The thing screamed and spat at them, hobbling ungracefully on its stubby legs.

"Sorry, mate," Jack apologized, now out of the beast's reach. It might have been a master of the sky, but on the ground it was so slow a baby could have out-toddled it. "You just didn't have the gams."

"We'll need to somehow lure two at once," Fitzwilliam declared, sword in his hand again. He waved it slowly back and forth.

"Shouldn't be a problem," Jack agreed, looking at all of the pterosaurs that were now circling above. Hundreds of them, it looked like. He took off his hat and began waving it again.

It wasn't a minute before one came diving down furiously at Fitzwilliam—another one right on its tail.

"Jump!" Jack cried.

Fitzwilliam grabbed the thing's claws and bellowed in triumph as it took off with him over the edge. Jack grabbed the second one— holding on tight to his bandana.

"Ahoy, permission to come aboard?" he asked, grinning.

Though it now had an unexpected passenger, the pterosaur ignored him.

After a moment, Jack realized why. And *why* it had been flying so close to the first. With a terrible, reptilian scream, it reached its neck out and slashed at the other pterosaur's tail with its toothy beak.

Fitzwilliam and Jack had gotten themselves into the middle of an Uglybird fight.

Fitzwilliam's beast worked its muscles hard and somersaulted in the air. The nobleman's son had to hold on to the claws for dear life as the earth and sky spun beneath him.

His beast came back up *under* Jack's, front claws out, screaming with anger.

Jack's paused in midair, beating its wings almost in a backward motion, to hold steady and meet the attack. It whipped its neck back and forth, trying to find an opening.

"Hey! Control your beastie there, Fitzy!" Jack cried out as his own reeled back from a blow.

"I believe, Jack, it was *your* pterosaur who started it!" Fitzwilliam countered, pulling his legs out of the way as Jack's began to grab at anything fleshy.

The two boys held on as tightly as they

could, trying not to look down. Their respective pterosaurs clawed and bit at each other, locked in deadly aerial combat.

"Must look pretty spectacular from the ground," Jack mused.

Too bad he wasn't down there to see it. He tried kicking the two beasts apart, but it was useless. He and Fitzwilliam might as well have been gnats for all the two creatures paid any attention to them.

Then Fitzwilliam's did another clever maneuver: it bit the other pterosaur's *wing* and pulled.

The injured pterosaur screamed as flesh was stripped from bone and cartilage. Scales peeled back and ripped. Jack and his beast began to plummet to Earth, the creature howling like an angry siren as they dropped.

"Fitzy!' Jack cried out. "DO SOME-THING!"

The nobleman's son thought fast. His own pterosaur was calm now, watching his enemy fall to its death. Fitzwilliam seized the opportunity to grab its neck. He swung forward and launched himself up over the beast's shoulder like a horseman. He landed, somewhat awkwardly, in the middle of its broad, scaly back.

There was no place for his legs with the giant wings beating up and down. Fitzwilliam was forced to kneel, gripping the creature with his knees. The pterosaur bucked for a moment, unhappy about what was going on atop its back. But Fitzwilliam kept his balance and hold.

"Easy there," he coaxed it, just as he did with his old mount. "Easy now . . ."

For lack of a bridle or bit, he reached down and grabbed each of the beast's wings . . . and pulled.

The pterosaur responded beautifully, as if it had been trained for this all its life. Fitzwilliam dug his knees in. "DIVE!" he ordered, pulling both wings, again.

The pterosaur dove.

It was a horrible game of catch-up.

Jack and his beast had separated from each other, and now each was falling free, tumbling end over end. Jack was frantically moving his arms and legs: he was either trying to slow his fall or discover the secret of flight, whichever happened first.

"Faster!" Fitzwilliam urged his flying steed.

It folded its wings almost entirely shut, dropping like a cannonball toward Jack.

The ground rushed up ever closer.

Jack continued to fall.

And then, just inches above the tree line, Fitzwilliam's beast broke into a swan dive. It gracefully caught Jack on its back. Leaves and branches thwacked against its curled-up claws as it skimmed over the jungle.

Jack held a hand to his heart and tried hard to breathe.

"You are welcome," Fitzwilliam said smugly.

The two boys and their Uglybird (who suddenly didn't look so ugly) flew over the island.

"Look, over there, a field close to the port," Fitzwilliam pointed out a few airborne moments later. "I will set us down there."

"Aye," Jack said, glad he was alive but a bit disappointed *he* wasn't flying the beastie.

At Fitzwilliam's urging the pterosaur slowed down and circled once before landing in the middle of a field.

"Good Bessie," Fitzwilliam said, patting it again on its haunch. He and Jack leaped down. The nobleman's son couldn't help preening a bit. "Well, I did do quite a good job back there. And getting us here. Do you not agree, *Captain* Jack Sparrow?"

"Oh, shove it, mate," Jack said, squinting his eyes at something moving at the edge of the field. "I don't exactly think your choice of landing strips was the best."

Jack's eyes widened, and Fitzwilliam turned quickly to see what Jack was staring at. With a horrified gasp, both boys froze, not knowing whether to run or stand still. Whatever they chose, it seemed they were done for—again.

CHAPTER FIVE

*I*t was a scene straight out of Jack's worst nightmare.

No, wait—Jack thought carefully. His worst nightmare was a lot *more* deadly than this. And it involved a certain Pirate Lord from Singapore and a certain tentacled captain. This, however, was still rather scary. A whole pack of oversize Constances surrounded them. They had long, matted fur and ridiculously huge claws: yellowed and sharp and several inches long. But it was their teeth that really did it. Huge, long, ivory tusks like an elephant's—but razor sharp.

They advanced, circling the two boys and the pterosaur. Some roared and others howled, their teeth flashing in the sunlight.

"Nice kitty," Jack said weakly. The cat closest to him growled in response.

"They are hunting as a *pack*," Fitzwilliam said, voice trembling with fear.

"Thank you for that interesting scientific fact," Jack said sarcastically.

The cats paced to-and-fro, tightening the circle with every step.

The pterosaur shifted nervously on its back feet. It placed its talons on the ground to steady itself, hoisting its wings up over its back.

Then, the lead cat sprang.

"Here we go!" Jack cried, drawing his

cutlass. Jack slashed, and the cat yowled and ripped the air with its giant paws, then fell heavily to the ground.

It stuck out its neck and roared at Fitzwilliam, trying to bite him.

Two more cat-things were already launching themselves at Jack. On the other side, one had begun to swipe at the pterosaur.

The pterosaur screamed a horrible, reptilian call and struck at the cat with its sharp beak.

"Guess he can take care of himself, then," Jack reasoned. "Or her. Self. Herself. Mustn't be chauvinistic about these things. Take help wherever one can get it."

Two more cats drew close. Jack leaped into the air, flipping forward over their backs and landing on a tree stump behind them.

"Over here, boys," he said, waving.

The cats screamed in confusion. They

spun around to face him—and cracked their skulls against each other.

Roaring in anger, the one on the left took its claw and raked the other one across the face. The one on the right hissed and bit the other one's ear.

Soon they were entangled in a horrible, bloody struggle in the dust.

"Cat fight!" Jack called encouragingly.

But another cat had already broken ranks: it was a young, eager-looking one with bright yellow eyes. Opening its mouth, it sprang at Jack, baring giant fangs.

Jack waited until the last second—

—and stepped aside. Casually.

Unable to stop its forward momentum, the cat crashed into the stump, burying its ridiculously sharp teeth deep into the dead wood. It growled and shook its head from side to side, but couldn't pull free.

"I'd go see a dentist about that, mate," Jack recommended.

Meanwhile, Fitzwilliam was doing his best against one of the bigger cats. It parried his blade with its claws almost like a human opponent—a much, *much* stronger one. It whacked Fitzwilliam's sword aside again and again with powerful blows that sent him reeling.

One knocked the aristocrat over, smashing his head against a large boulder.

The cat roared in triumph, rearing back for the killing bite.

But the "boulder" was, in actuality, the pterosaur. It whipped its head around and sliced its beak across the attacking cat's exposed neck.

"Would you look at that?" Jack said, whistling. "By Davy Jones's Locker—no, wait," he thought for a second, no longer wanting to invoke the dread captain's name. "By the Seven Seas! I think Drag is actually *helping* us!"

Fitzwilliam looked confused for a moment. "Who is 'Drag'?"

Jack rolled his eyes. Once again, the utter stupidity of others amazed him. "Your mount? Drag, as in *Dragon*? The big lizardy flying thing we hitched a ride here on?"

Drag gave a triumphant scream. It almost seemed to smile.

"Good show, there!" the nobleman's son said, grinning. He patted it on its flank. "Well done!"

Jack looked around at the remaining cats. There were at least twenty of them left. Far too many for the two boys to fight off, even with the pterosaur helping them. He looked at Drag with a critical eye. Even if he—or she—couldn't take off easily with the two of them on him—or her—maybe they would escape the worst blows up on its back.

"Fitzy!" Jack called. "As before! All aboard the beastie!"

Fitzwilliam turned to clamber up over the pterosaur's neck. But turning his back to the cats was a bad idea. One of them leaped up. Fitzwilliam tried to pull himself out of the way—but his feet still dangled. The cat swiped out with its claw but missed Fitzwilliam.

Three more cats broke rank and charged him. Jack sheathed his sword; one or two cats he could have handled. But not three. Not without another sword maybe, or a dagger, and a musket, and a cannon. . . . Basically, it was time for a strategic retreat.

"YARRRRRRRRRRGGGGGGGGGH!" he screamed, running for Drag.

Fitzwilliam was now seated on the pterosaur's back. He put a hand out, ready to help Jack up. The captain of the *Barnacle* leaped, putting all of his strength into it.

It wasn't enough.

A cat jumped up at him. It clapped its paws together, catching his arm and pulling him right out of the air.

"Jack!" Fitzwilliam cried. Their hands touched, but didn't hold. Jack fell.

Right in the middle of the remaining cats.

Drag kept whipping its neck out, snapping at this and that one. But there were too many, advancing too quickly.

Jack drew his sword again and began to slash with all his skill and might.

He spun and jumped and parried and thrusted . . . but there were still too many attacking at once.

"This is a rotten way for ol' Jack to end," he muttered. "Eaten by a bunch of over-grown house cats with dental problems."

A shadow fell over the land. A strong wind rose.

"What now?" Jack demanded. "More of this 'dancing hours' business? Is it suddenly leap year? An eclipse?"

"No, Jack, look!" Fitzwilliam pointed up.

Weaving in formation so tightly that they blocked out the sun, was the largest flock of pterosaurs the two had seen yet. Hundreds of them it seemed, huge and green and gray and screaming.

"Like vultures," Fitzwilliam said, shivering. "Waiting for the kill!"

"I don't think so, Fitzy," Jack said slowly. They seemed to be eyeing the *cats*, not the two boys. What must have been the leader screamed out. It looked a lot like Drag. Same shape wings, same length tail . . .

"By Calypso's earrings," Jack swore, laughing. "That's Drag's da! Or mum," he added.

As one, the pterosaurs dove and attacked.
The cats hissed and yowled in response.

It was one of the weirdest, bloodiest
battles in history—or at least in Isla
Esquelética's history. Pterosaurs tore at cats
with their beaks and their talons. Cats
hissed and leaped, attacking with their claws
and teeth. The pterosaurs made a ring
around Drag, protecting him. Or her.

Fitzwilliam and Jack watched for a
moment, transfixed. Then Jack tugged on
Fitzwilliam's shirtsleeve.

"I think that's our cue to leave, mate," he
said quietly. It was true: neither cat *nor*
pterosaur was paying attention to them.
Even Drag was too busy saying hello to
friends and fighting off the cats.

Fitzwilliam slipped down off Drag's back
and gave him—or her—a friendly pat good-
bye. Then the two boys quickly and silently

slipped away. They tried not to listen, but the piercing sounds of screams, roars, and hisses followed them until they were halfway over the next rise.

Jack pulled out the pocket watch. He frowned when he saw the dial. "That cost us over an hour, mate. Means we have only ten and a half to set things back to normal. . . . Are you even *listening*?" he shouted, frustrated.

But Fitzwilliam wasn't listening at all. He was staring slack-jawed out to sea. Jack squinted and looked. There was the *Flying Dutchman*, still stubbornly moored offshore under a sky that was half-day, half-night. Surrounding the cursed vessel was a fleet of three tall ships. All flew a blue flag with three white seagulls.

"Nice ships," Jack said appreciatively. "But what's got you so moony-faced?"

"That is the family crest of the explorer

Leonardo Leone!" Fitzwilliam said with awe. "He sailed these waters over *two hundred years* ago. We are watching history as it *happens*, Jack! He was the one who discovered these islands!"

"Well, it looks like the island has discovered *him*, too. More to the point, Stone-Eyed Sam has," Jack said, pointing. Island warriors had boarded the boats and were taking their crews captive.

What a lucky break! With Jones surrounded by famous historical figures, and famous historical figures all being hauled off by crazy men with glass weapons, *no one* was going to care about ol' Jack and Fitzy now!

But suddenly Jack realized something. "We've got to stop them! We've got to make sure Leonardo and his crew . . . explore all of the . . . explory places that they do. Make the history they're supposed to!"

Fitzwilliam gave Jack a suspicious look. "Day is night, the dead are living, flying dragons battle demonic cats . . . why does this *one thing* upset you compared to all of the other problems you have caused with the flow of time?"

"We, mate, we. *We* caused. Your watch, my fiddling. It was a partnership," Jack countered. "If Leone is hurt, or hypnotized, or killed, or eaten, or what-have-you, and doesn't return to Spain, Europeans won't find the small group of islands at the western edge of the East Indies. Like this one, for instance. At least not for some time."

"So?" Fitzwilliam demanded. "Again, what do *you* care? I did not think either history *or* geography were your strong points."

"Purely selfish reasons, mate," Jack said. "If the tales Da told me were true—and who really knows, what with the rum and all—I have some grand-kin who met somewhere near Tortuga."

He looked at Fitzwilliam expectantly. But the nobleman's son still looked confused, not understanding.

Jack sighed. He spoke very slowly.

"If I can't save Leone, I might wipe out my own existence! If there is no Leonardo Leone, there is no Isla Esquelética, no Tortuga . . . *NO JACK SPARROW*. Savvy?"

CHAPTER SIX

*F*itzwilliam thought over Jack's words for a moment before finally understanding.

"That is a very interesting philosophical question, Jack," he finally said. "You mean there is a chance that what *you* did—with *my* pocket watch—might in effect prevent you from ever having been born?"

"That's about the size of it there, mate," Jack said gravely. "I might have accidentally killed my own grandmother. Or grandfather. Or grand-uncle. Some very important early Sparrow who would no longer be able to beget whoever was going to beget *me*. I'd vanish like I'd never existed."

Fitzwilliam didn't look like he was as concerned as he should have been. Jack frowned and whacked him on the arm.

"Come *on*. No time for jokes. We have to go save Leone!" He pulled his shirt together and hiked up his belt, preparing to march down to the docks and save the day.

"Wait," Fitzwilliam said.

The tone in his voice made Jack stop.

"Think about it. It is just as important to set time straight—perhaps more so. And we only have ten or so hours to do that."

"How do you figure that, mate?" Jack demanded, suspicious.

"If we do what Chantico says and set time straight, everything will go back to the way it was," Fitzwilliam explained patiently.

"Stone-Eyed Sam will be dead again, those horrible cats and our friendly pterosaurs will disappear (along with the unfriendly ones), and Leonardo will be back to where he was, sailing the blue seas without Davy Jones or Stone-Eyed Sam bothering him. If we waste time saving just Leone we may run out of time to fix . . . er . . . time. And then the goddess will come and destroy us. '*Savvy*'?"

Jack ignored the dig and thought about what Fitzwilliam had said. It made sense.

"All right, then. There's only one thing to do. And it means going back into the water."

"*BACK?*" Fitzwilliam shrieked. "We *abandoned* the *Barnacle*. . . . You *tied me to a totem pole* and *paddled me* to this *wretched island* because Davy Jones can only set foot on land once every ten years! We walked *all the way* to this other wretched port . . ."

"Not all the way," Jack pointed out

helpfully. "You're forgetting the part where we were sucked up by waterspouts and went flying on Drag."

". . . Flying lizards . . . giant cats . . . my hair nearly *ruined* . . ." Fitzwilliam sputtered, almost incoherently.

Jack waited patiently for Fitzwilliam to stop his hysterics.

"Are you through yet?" he asked brightly.

"Yes," Fitzwilliam sighed, defeated.

"We need help," Jack explained. "I don't know how to fix this blasted watch of yours. I'm guessing that none of the friends we've made on the island—such as cats, lizards, Aztec warriors, volcano goddesses, and good ol' Torrents—would help us even if they *knew* how to help us. We need *big* help. *Magical* help. *Tia Dalma* help."

Fitzwilliam gulped. The few times he had met the mystic were scary enough. She was beautiful but creepy—funny but frightening. The last time he'd encountered her, outside of New Orleans, she had marked his neck with what looked like a crab tattoo, and told him it would only be removed when he returned to her what was lost to him.* That was something else she had a way with, speaking in incoherent riddles. Fitzwilliam wasn't sure he really *wanted* to meet her again.

But he didn't have any other ideas.

"You're right," he admitted grudgingly.

"And to see *her*, we need a boat," Jack sighed. "Always with the water. Swamps, marshes, beaches . . . never understood that about her. . . . Anyway, it's back to the *Barnacle*. Stealthylike, this time."

Which was how yet again Jack found himself tromping through the sweaty island jungle.

* In Vol. 6, *Silver*.

A very *lively* jungle now, with time going all funny, and certainly *not* standing still. He slapped the gnats on his neck, ignored the fact that the night sky and shining sun were simultaneously above him, and stepped around the weird little mouse-things with horns on their backs that occasionally scuttled past.

As they got closer to shore, the two boys also had to avoid the other strange inhabitants of the island: the warriors (fairskinned, light-eyed sailors who had been hypnotized by Stone-Eyed Sam into believing they were Aztecs). Bands of them roamed the island, still looking for Jack and Fitzwilliam.

The two boys hunkered down in the tall sea grass that grew near the beach and tried to quietly slip through. But the blades of grass were sharp and stiff and rubbed against each other noisily.

"SHHH!" Jack hushed Fitzwilliam.

But then Jack stepped on a dead crab, whose shell made a magnificent cracking noise.

"SHHH, yourself!" Fitzwilliam whispered back.

A pair of warriors came rushing over and looked around. The two boys froze. A warrior prodded the grass with his spear. Fitzwilliam had to maneuver and jump back and forth like a dancer to avoid its tip.

Jack had to stop himself from laughing out loud at the sight.

Eventually the two warriors moved on.

Jack and Fitzwilliam crept to the water's edge. The *Barnacle* was still there, rocking gently on the waves. Jack's heart swelled with pride when he saw her.

But then that selfsame heart sank when Jack realized how much open water was between him and his beloved boat. On this side of the island, where it was sunny daytime, the sky was clear and the ocean almost flat, they would be visible for miles.

There was an old skiff drawn on shore, which would be useful for getting to the *Barnacle*. . . . But Jack stopped Fitzwilliam as he began to shove the little boat over the sand to the water.

"If we start rowing our way out there, we'll be sitting ducks for the entire world to see," Jack pointed out. "Every Uglybird, *insane* sea captain with storm powers, brain-washed 'Aztec,' *undead* sea captain with *sword* powers, unfriendly native volcano goddess, and *slimy*, *tentacled* sea captain will be able to see us. And do that thing where they, you know, *get* us."

"You do have a point," Fitzwilliam said. "But what can we do? Even if you could swim the whole distance, they would still see us."

Jack didn't miss the fact that Fitzwilliam

had said "you." The nobleman's son probably fancied himself a stellar swimmer.

Jack could swim. If he had to. In a pinch.

"Always coming up with downsides, never solutions. Not much of an ideas-man are you, Fitzy? Thank goodness for ol' Jack and his brains," he said, praising himself. "Here's what we'll do, mate. We'll turn this little boat here right over, aye? Then we'll walk *under the water* with it, keeping it over our heads *with a pocket of air for us to breathe!*"

The plan had leaped to his mind full-blown. It was strange, almost like he had somehow thought it all through at some point before.

"That is the stupidest idea I have ever heard," Fitzwilliam declared. "It will never work."

"No, it really will," Jack said, getting a strange look on his face. "Trust me . . . I think I've done it before. Or maybe after.

Some other time. I've definitely done it. Somewhen."

Ironically, something about the way Jack hesitated made Fitzwilliam believe it. Jack certainly wasn't acting like his usual, lying-by-the-seat-of-his-pants self.

As quickly as they could, they hoisted the skiff up over their heads—and walked into the sea. Jack was in front, of course, so Fitzwilliam had to trust that he knew where they were going.

Walking was difficult. The underwater sand was deep and mucky, and it was very slow going. The small pocket of air under the boat became stale and smelled very, very bad, very, very quickly.

At one point, Jack was positive that a small school of squid tried to nibble at his knees.

Another time, an eerie large gathering of pure white crabs scuttled past them, clacking their claws, with black eyes fixed on some unknown destination.

But Jack's sense of direction was spot on: they almost tripped over the anchor and rope of the *Barnacle*. They carefully put the skiff aside and swam up the rope, throwing themselves overboard quickly, so as not to attract any attention.

"By grace, that has done it!" Fitzwilliam cheered as they hauled up the anchor.

Jack grinned and stood behind the wheel, the only place he really felt right. He had a very powerful, strange sense of déjà vu. He shook his head to free himself of it.

The two boys turned to wave good-bye to Isla Esquelética, giddy about having made it off the island.

The scene they were leaving sobered them some, however. The sky was divided neatly down the middle of the island, with

stars and dark sky blanketing one side, and golden sun pouring down on the other. Jack stood on the Barnacle's bowsprit and surveyed the island. The volcano was puffing angry black smoke. Flocks of pterosaurs hovered in the sky. Clouds roiled at the edge of the horizon, blowing backward and making strange, ugly shapes. A hollow wind blew.

"It is like the apocalypse. The end of the world," Fitzwilliam said softly.

"Whatever, mate. At least we're free from it!" Jack smiled smugly. His plan with the skiff was brilliant, and they were free. . . . All was good with the world. Thanks to him.

And then a loud, ominous thudding noise came from behind them.

Fitzwilliam and Jack looked at each other, then slowly turned around.

And there, his tentacles twitching, stood Davy Jones.

CHAPTER SEVEN

Jack grinned one of his especially irritating grins. It was a grin of complete and absolute smugness. It started in the middle of his mouth and worked slowly out to the edges, curling up the ends of his lips.

Fitzwilliam began to get nervous. It didn't pay to be smug around a powerful creature like Davy Jones.

"Welcome aboard, mate," Jack said. He tipped his hat at a jaunty angle. "Although once again I was not asked permission. One captain to another. It's just basic politeness."

"As *one captain to another*," Davy Jones growled, his words bubbling. "I'm thinkin' about sending ye to the bottom of the sea."

"Oh, I don't think you'll be doing that," Jack said casually. "I don't think you'd ever hurt me . . . as long as I have the watch!"

Fitzwilliam and Jones both expected Jack to pull out the pocket watch triumphantly and wave it in the tentacled captain's face. But for once he was showing a little restraint. Instead, he cupped it protectively in his hands—just in case any tentacles whipped out and tried to grab it.

Jack couldn't help looking at the dial. Only eight hours left! They didn't have time to be mucking about with the cursed sea captain. . . .

Davy Jones was too furious to reply. The tips of his tentacles curled and writhed in anger. His weird eyes filled with demonic light.

Jack took one step backward. Behind Fitzwilliam.

Jones shook himself and tapped his staff on the deck.

"It matters not. I have everything I need," he said, more to himself than the two boys. He frowned in concentration. "All that is left is to lock 'em up for safekeeping. Until the time is right."

He rapped on the deck again with his staff. Out of the shadows came two horrible creatures. They were part-human, like Jones . . . but just barely. One scuttled sideways and clacked "hands" above his head that were really ugly, bumpy claws. Instead of normal eyes, he glared at them from two eyestalks that twitched above his brow. The other sailor was slimy and thin, with almost no arms at all. His mouth was a lipless circle ringed with triangular teeth.

"Eyech," Jack couldn't help saying. "The crab I get, but what's the other? Remora? Eel? Some sort of other wierd sea thingy?"

Before he and Fitzwilliam could even get to their swords two more cursed sailors appeared behind them, grabbing their arms. Jack shook the watch to get Jones's attention.

"I'll drop it, I will, I'll crush it if you lay a hand—er, claw—er, fin—on my head. *Our* heads," he added after Fitzwilliam glared at him.

"Oh, *do* be careful with them," Jones cooed sarcastically to his crew. "Treat them with all the respect they deserve—from *one captain to another*."

Clouds boiled on the horizon. The *Flying Dutchman* appeared out of the darkness next to the *Barnacle*. The cursed crew set up a gangplank between the two ships. Jack and Fitzwilliam were shoved forward as the fishy sailors laughed, creaked, and made other horrible noises.

The two boys tried to keep brave faces as they were forced belowdecks. But the *Flying Dutchman* was nightmarish. From the smell—everything seemed to be rotting—to the sounds of the crew making their way wordlessly around the ship—to the very bulkheads themselves. Between the coral and old shells and bones, Jack swore he saw a pair of eyes open and blink at him. He shuddered.

But the brig was more or less like any other ship's brig: dark, damp, and locked.

"This is all your fault!" Fitzwilliam cried the moment their captors had left.

"Now, now, Fitzy, don't get your breeches in a twist," Jack said comfortingly. "Look at it this way, mate: we'll be the first *living* sailors to have ever boarded the *Flying Dutchman* . . . and gotten back off again!"

"You are assuming quite a lot there, Jack," Fitzwilliam pointed out. "Especially the part where we manage to *get off again*."

"I'll think of something. Don't you worry," Jack promised.

"That is exactly what *makes* me worry. You 'thinking' of something!" Fitzwilliam shot back.

"Ahh, listen to the two lovebirds," a haunting voice came from behind them. "I'm surprised you made it *this* far together."

The two boys turned. Standing in the shadows was none other than Tia Dalma!

She revealed her creepy blue-stained-tooth smile at them. Fitzwilliam put his hand to his neck, touching the crab mark she had placed there.

"Fancy meeting you here," Jack said,

trying not to look surprised. "Coincidentally, we were just on our way to find you."

Tia Dalma snatched the watch out of Jack's hand.

"Hmm. Wonder why Jones did not try that," Fitzwilliam observed. Jack glared at him.

"Ah, there it is!" Tia Dalma breathed. She held the watch up delicately between two fingers, like it was an egg. "What was lost from you was found again."

"No offense, milady," Jack said, interrupting what sounded like the beginning of one of her long, creepy speeches. "But you seem awful *calm* considering where we all are. In whose boat I mean. The man with the tentacles, is what I'm saying. Who has us all captured."

But Tia Dalma just ignored him.

"This watch holds great power, witty Jack," she continued.

"Yes, yes, we know all that," Jack said

impatiently. Sometimes Tia Dalma could take a while to get to the point.

Then she frowned, noticing the hands of the watch. An even darker shadow fell over the brig. There was something scary and powerful about Tia Dalma. Almost like Chantico.

"Jaaaack," she drew out his name. "Have you been *playing* wit' this t'ing?"

"No," Jack answered immediately.

Fitzwilliam rolled his eyes. Tia Dalma glared at him.

"*Jack*," she prodded.

"Maybe a little," he admitted. He held his finger and thumb closely together, to show her *how* little.

"JACK!"

Her voice rang out. Her eyes flashed. The two boys could feel power building in the room. Angry power.

"Fine. Quite a lot, then," Jack said peevishly.

"The hours have been dancing, though the hands are now still," she observed.

Fitzwilliam mouthed the words questioningly at Jack. What did she mean? After all, the hands *were* moving—back to 12. Jack shrugged and made a "crazy" gesture, twirling his finger next to his head.

"Your time is running out, Jack Sparrow. This will be a greater task than it should have been," Tia Dalma continued, shaking her head.

"What's that supposed to mean?" Jack demanded.

Tia Dalma smiled and shook the watch. "This has a great history behind it, Jack. It was . . . *discovered* not long after the last gathering of the Brethren Court of Pirate Lords."

"The Brethren *what* of Pirate *who*?" Fitz-william demanded.

Jack shushed him. It looked like she was actually about to impart some important information—a rare thing for her to do. For free, anyway.

"De pirate Tartaglia had it first. Him was a little man, more thief than sailor . . . but him sensed its power. Him used de watch as a false Piece of Eight to fool other pirates into believing *him* was a Pirate Lord."

"*What Piece of Eight? How could anyone mistake that watch for a coin? And how does that make you a Pirate Lord?*" Fitzwilliam whispered. Jack shushed him again. If only Arabella were here. She could explain things to the aristocrat . . . and she would be thrilled to learn about these legends firsthand!

"But what Tartaglia did not know was its true power. The watchmaker who made it was also an alchemist. Him made it so the watch could do more than tell time—him made it so it could alter time itself." She pointed up at the deck above them. "Eventually, Davy Jones heard about it. De poor, brokenhearted spirit believed him could harness its powers for him own use."

This time, both Fitzwilliam *and* Jack looked at each other: brokenhearted spirit? The evil, tentacled thing that had thrown them all in here had a heart?

"Him believed he could use it to return to the moment when him true love, the goddess Calypso . . . *disappeared from him.* Him would go and prevent her from doing so." She sashayed slowly across the room to Jack. "The watch has been kept hidden from Jones for many long years . . . until *now* . . ."

She glared at him, her face just inches from his.

"What do we do to fix the watch?" he asked politely, unsure how this all fit in with his present predicament.

"There is only one way to stop the hours from dancing. You must find a person who doesn't belong in this present moment of time." She spoke without blinking. It was extremely unnerving.

Jack forced himself not to step backward. He smiled sheepishly. "Easy enough," he said, blustering. "Finding a mate who doesn't belong. The island's *crawling* with them. Be done by lunch."

"But there's more, Jack Sparrow," Tia Dalma whispered.

Jack sighed. "Of course there is."

"The person out of time must be standing under the moon and sun, and must be in possession of the watch—and then let it go *before it strikes the twelfth chime.* It must be removed from him grasp. If not, all of time will collapse on itself and doom and chaos will rule on dese Seven Seas."

"Er," Jack gulped.

"And if you choose the wrong person," she continued, "someone who *does* belong in dis present moment of time, time will remain warped forever."

"In other words, we must be very careful to whom we hand the watch," Fitzwilliam translated needlessly. "That might be a bit more difficult."

"Ah, yes, and it's complicated a teensy bit more," Jack pointed out sarcastically, "by the fact that we're *locked up on the ship* of the 'poor, brokenhearted spirit' Davy Jones."

"Who would just as soon drown Jack as take the watch," Fitzwilliam added.

"Aye," Jack added, a little testily.

"Leave that to me," Tia Dalma said with a mysterious smile.

"I hate it when she says that," Jack complained.

The mystic made her way over to the portside bulkhead. Like the rest of the ship, instead of wood, it was a nasty mishmash of bones and dead sea-things. She leaned forward, almost touching it with her lips, and whispered.

Several shells and pieces of seaweed slid aside and a dead-looking face appeared in the ship's hull.

Fitzwilliam and Jack recoiled in horror.

Tia Dalma again whispered, now in a language that neither boy understood.

With wet, creaking noises, the man in the hull moved out of the way, opening a hole in the ship's wall. Tia Dalma stood aside and gave the boys a triumphant smile.

Jack stuck his head out through the hole and looked down. It was a long way to the water . . . but their only hope.

Tia Dalma placed the watch in Jack's hand and closed his fingers around it.

"It is still my watch," Fitzwilliam mumbled. People seemed to keep forgetting that.

"See you on de other side, gentlemen," she drawled—then jumped.

"Blimey," Jack breathed. Then he turned and saluted Fitzwilliam, and also jumped. The nobleman followed, saying a quick prayer under his breath.

The three hit the water with a slap, and began swimming for their lives.

CHAPTER EIGHT

"*I* shall not be sorry," Jack heaved, pulling himself out of the water and onto the beach, "if I never cross that blasted piece of water again. First on a totem, then *under* a boat, and now swimming! What's next, I ask you? Traveling on the backs of sea turtles?"

He stomped up the sand and wrung out his bandana. What seemed lika a gallon of seawater poured from it. Jack thought about the creepy crew on the *Flying Dutchman* and shuddered.

Fitzwilliam and Tia Dalma came close behind.

Jack cast an appraising glance upward. The sun and moon were still both overhead in their separate portions of the sky. As clouds moved from east to west they changed colors and darkened so rapidly it made Jack dizzy. He shook his head.

"Well, we've got the first bit down," he said, pointing out the celestial bodies to Fitzwilliam and Tia Dalma. "We are under both sun and moon. All we need to do now is find the 'person out of time' to 'stand under the moon and sun.'"

A sudden scuffling noise came from behind the dunes.

In a moment, the silhouettes of angry warriors stood against the horizon.

As they came closer, however, the pinched noses and light eyes of the European sailors became obvious. Not to mention the occasional shiny boot or belt buckle under colorful native garb.

Their weaponry didn't look so silly, however. There were giant wooden shafts with obsidian blades embedded in them. Lances and spears as tall as the men themselves. Clubs and arrows and slings—all of which were encrusted with deadly black glass that glittered in the sun.

Jack and Fitzwilliam took a step back. But they were quickly surrounded. Behind them was the sea—and they were too exhausted to even consider escaping that way.

Only Tia Dalma stood her ground, swaying slightly, like she always did. With that same dreamy, creepy smile.

"What in blazes is the matter with you, woman," Jack demanded in a loud whisper. "How can you smile at a time like this?"

"But these are not warriors, Jack," she said. "These are honest sailors."

She raised her hand, spreading her fingers, and spoke something softly. Again, in a language neither Jack nor Fitzwilliam had ever heard.

Something passed over the warriors, like a shadow or a breeze.

They began to shake their heads and look around stupidly.

"Where—where am I?" one of them, befuddled, asked.

"It is like they are awaking from a dream, or a deep sleep," Fitzwilliam observed.

"I—I had just fallen overboard, we was attacked by the Spanish . . ." an English sailor said, putting his hand to his temple. But his fingers were blocked by the strange headdress he wore. "Bless me addled deadlights—are those *feathers*?"

"We were taking on water," said another sailor, with a similar dazed expression. He looked at the foreign weapon in his hands in confusion. "'Twas the merchant *Natalie*, full of rum and sugar. A wave knocked me over and I was gone to feed the fish for sure . . . What in the Seven Seas happened?"

All around them, the 'Aztecs' were recounting similar stories of being wrecked near the island. Some in sea battles, some by bad luck.

The chief sailor that Jack and Fitzwilliam had had the most dealings with was sitting on a rock, holding a jaguar pelt in his hand. Not long ago, he had ordered Jack and Fitzwilliam to be sacrificed to Chantico.* Now he just looked tired and frightened.

A couple of the other sailors still hung around him, as if waiting for orders.

* In Vol. 8, *The Timekeeper*.

"If ever a man didn't belong in a time and place, that would be him," Jack decided and marched proudly up to the man.

"Ah, beg pardon, mate, but would you mind holding this watch for ah—a minute or so? It's just that I need to . . . well, I have some personal things I must attend to." Jack said. He checked the sky: the moon and sun were both still out, above him.

"JACK," Tia Dalma shouted, suddenly at his side. Jack jumped. He hated when she did that. "Are you *sure* him the one? De person who doesn't belong in de present moment of time?"

"Well, of course. I mean, just *look* at him," Jack pointed.

The man in question was too busy to notice the offered watch: he was trying not to sneeze as another sailor helped him pull a feather out through a piercing that had been made in his nose's septum.

"At least the middle bit is gold," the helpful sailor said, holding up a gleaming golden bead still sticky with mucus.

"Just because Stone-Eyed Sam is dead in our time, that doesn't mean *he* is," Tia Dalma pointed out.

"But this entire city—the city of pirates—was all bones and destruction," Jack protested, remembering it from their first adventure.*

"So *he's* probably dead, too."

"Are you willing to risk all of time collapsing on 'probably,' Jack?" she asked.

"She has a point," Fitzwilliam put in.

"But how do you know about Stone-Eyed Sam?" Jack demanded, rounding on Tia Dalma. "I don't remember telling you any-

---

* Read Vol. 1, *The Coming Storm,* for the whole story of Stone-Eyed Sam's city.

thing about him being out and about here! And while we're asking questions, Davy Jones said he already had everything he needed, and 'all that was left is to lock 'em up for safekeeping.' 'Em.' As in 'them.' Besides us and, more important, the watch, *you* were the only thing locked up in his brig. Just how do *you* fit into his little time-traveling plans?"

Tia Dalma looked pained and confused.

"Now, you wanted me to hold something?" the most talkative sailor asked, now free of his nose stud. He eyed the golden watch a little too greedily. He might have been confused, recently hypnotized, and mostly naked, but he recognized a precious thing when he saw it.

Tia Dalma grabbed the watch from Jack, removing it from harm's way. She glanced at the dial.

"One hour left, Jack," she said, showing him the time on the watch.

"One hour?" Jack stammered. "Just how long were we aboard that bloody *Flying Dutchman*?"

"Time have a funny way aboard de *Dutchman*, too, Jack," Tia Dalma replied. "Best get going. An hour is not long."

The three looked at each other, and without a word they began to tiptoe off, away from the beach. The poor, confused men would just have to figure things out for themselves. Jack had bigger problems to fix.

They ran along the paths in the jungle that, before time went all wonky, were littered with bones and the remains of dead pirates. Now they were freshly laid and well-kept. And instead of discovering the pirate city by literally falling into it through a crumbling wall,* the three "friends" were

* As they had in Vol. 1, *The Coming Storm*.

able to approach it up a wide, well-maintained avenue.

People were bustling about their daily life, paying the three of them no mind. Kids were playing outside, women were hanging wash, and a cat was chasing a pigeon on a roof.

"For a lost pirate kingdom this actually seems like a very pleasant place to live," Fitzwilliam commented.

They headed toward the palace—trying to remember all the bobby traps that they had encountered the first time they were there.

"Well, in we go, then," Fitzwilliam said, heading for the steps. Jack stopped him, and pointed. Entering the palace in front of them was none other than Captain Torrents!

He stepped carefully, as if he also knew all about the island's booby traps. But not *too* carefully. After all, he could summon a whirlwind to save him from falling.

Jack waited until the pirate was inside and then motioned for the three of them to follow. Lacking the ability to conjure up storms on a whim, they had to be a good deal more careful.

"Ah, it's like a trip down memory lane," Jack whispered as they inched along the walls.

The going was slow: beside the traps, they now had to deal with any warriors whose minds had not yet been freed by Tia Dalma. The warriors marched along the corridors in pairs like castle guards. Castle guards with obsidian weapons and jade jewelry. They did not seem to be bothered by Torrents and left him alone. And so, Jack and the others followed.

The big, stormy captain finally made it to the throne room. Jack, Fitzwilliam, and Tia Dalma crouched behind a giant chest filled with treasure and waited to see what would happen.

The mad pirate king sat on his throne, with the powerful Sword of Cortés across his lap, unsheathed. His right hand lay upon the pommel. He was looking upward and chanting.

Jack and his friends also looked up. There, suspended over a pit of what looked like boiling lava, locked in a giant cage, was Leonardo Leone and his crew.

Jack gulped. It looked dangerous. One false move and *splat*—there went his history.

But the sailors weren't trying to escape. They looked kind of dazed, in fact. Their eyes were half-closed, and some of them were humming along to the chanting by the pirate king.

"Ahoy, there," Stone-Eyed said, looking away from his captives and greeting

Torrents. His stone eye glittered eerily in the torchlight. "My warriors have told tell of you. You'll make a fine addition to my army, what with your ability to control the tempers of the Earth. In fact, I was just in the middle of . . . *indoctrinating* some new troops."

"I'm not here to join you and your motley bag," Torrents rumbled like the thunder he could summon. His eyes began to flash. "I'm here to collect something that doesn't rightly belong to you. *The Sword of Cortés,*" Torrents explained. "None other than Davy Jones appointed me to retrieve it. So it'd be best if you just handed it over, politely, and I'll be on my way."

"Not on your thrice-accursed hide!" Stone-Eyed roared, leaping up with the sword.

Torrents grinned and pulled his own sword. It was obvious he had been expecting a fight—and looking forward to it.

Stone-Eyed Sam brought the fabled Sword down, muttering something as he did. It glowed red and flashed. Torrents parried with his own cutlass—and then sent little bolts of lightning along it for good measure.

A wind rose up, putting out most of the torches in the room. Tia Dalma freed the remaining 'Aztecs,' and most fled the throne room. In the semidarkness the two powerful pirates fought back and forth, their swords clanging. The air itself was lit on fire from the magic being wielded: electric blue, fiery red, an angry, ghoulish green.

Stone-Eyed Sam pointed the Sword of Cortés at Torrents. Bolts of energy flew at his head. Torrents threw his hand up: an angry black cloud appeared between them, swallowing all the magic.

Stone-Eyed Sam roared and swung the

Sword again like a normal weapon. Torrents ducked to avoid the blow. It hit the stone wall behind him with a mighty clang. Chunks of rock went flying.

"That is *such* a nice sword." Jack sighed.

"How much time do we have left?" Fitzwilliam whispered, ignoring Jack.

"Twenty minutes," Tia Dalma answered mechanically, without even looking at the watch.

Jack had to do something. Quick.

Stone-Eyed Sam *definitely* didn't belong in the present moment of time. He was one of the few people on the whole island that Jack was positive should have been dead—he had seen his skeleton himself!

There was, of course, also the explorer hanging from the ceiling—Leonardo Leone . . . who should have died at least two hundred years ago. But he was a lot harder to get to, what with being in a cage up above a pit.

Then Jack remembered. If it were to be Stone-Eyed, he would have to be outside, under the moon and sun.

Jack leaped up and started waving.

"Hey! Stoney! Look-it! It's your old mate, Jack! Whoo-hoo! Over here!"

"What in blazes are you doing, Jack?" Fitzwilliam hissed.

"Trying to attract Mr. Undead's attention. To lure him outside," Jack explained.

But what Jack forgot was that *both* pirates—Stone-Eyed Sam *and* Torrents—had a score to settle with him.

They stopped their fighting and turned on Jack.

Jack gulped.

Stone-Eyed pointed the Sword and shot a bolt of energy at him. Torrents held his fists out and cast lightning at him.

Jack threw himself aside, barely avoiding both lethal dangers.

Torrents took advantage of Stone-Eyed Sam's momentary distraction and tried to swipe at him with a sword.

Stone-Eyed responded by chanting something. The Sword of Cortés glowed green, and crackling embers launched themselves at Torrents.

Jack, Tia Dalma, and Fitzwilliam dove for cover.

Jack popped up again like a rabbit.

"Remember me? Over here!"

Stone-Eyed barely looked over, tossing a bolt of energy at him with the tip of the Sword. Jack rolled out of the way . . . and almost right into the small cyclone Torrents had summoned.

"This is getting ridiculous," he muttered. Fitzwilliam was helping Tia Dalma clamber behind a stone bench: nasty little bits of the supernatural were now loose all over the room.

Jack drew his sword and leaped into the fray, hoping to get Stone-Eyed Sam's attention with a well-aimed blow. But nothing too damaging; he still had to get the pirate to chase him outside.

Jack quickly brought up his cutlass and used its gold tip to slice across the top of the mad pirate's pants. The cloth tore and pulled away, revealing brightly colored knickers beneath.

Stone-Eyed Sam hissed with rage and shot fiery bolts at Jack. But then he turned and deflected an attack from Torrents of three little dust devils aimed at his throat.

"No sense of dignity at all," Jack sniffed, hopping as the fiery bolts hit the floor near his feet. The pirate didn't really care about his exposed knickers. He just wanted to kill Torrents—*and* Jack.

"Jack," Fitzwilliam called out. "We do not have much time!"

Jack gave him an exasperated look. "What does it look like I'm doin', mate? Mending my nets?"

A tiny lightning bolt struck him on his backside. He leaped, trying to keep from screaming. His own pants smoked a little.

Watching the two pirates, his eyes narrowed. There was only one thing Stone-Eyed Sam seemed to care about besides getting Jack and Torrents.

The Sword of Cortés.

Jack quickly jumped in between the two powerful pirates. He slashed his cutlass out at Stone-Eyed, slicing him across his sword hand—

—and grabbed the Sword of Cortés as the pirate dropped it, howling.

Jack had to admit: for all the trouble it had

caused him, it felt *good* to finally hold the Sword again.*

Quick as a sparrow, Jack made for the door. His arms flailed as he pranced away. Fitzwilliam and Tia Dalma quickly took off after him.

So did Stone-Eyed Sam.

And so did Torrents.

"Chin up, Leo!" Jack called back to the explorer and his poor captive crew. "Stay there and if everything goes to plan, time will go back to normal, you'll go back to your right era (or is it epoch?), and Jack Sparrow will be born right proper!"

---

* To see "all the trouble it had caused him," be sure to read Vol. 4, *The Sword of Cortés.*

CHAPTER NINE

*U*nder a sunny day and sparkling night, outside a lost pirate city full of people who should have been dead, Jack Sparrow fought for his life against the two pirates.

With his cutlass in his left hand and the Sword of Cortés in his right, he parried and ducked desperately.

Even without his powerful sword, Stone-Eyed Sam was a dangerous opponent. He was clearly raving mad. From his belt he pulled two glittering jeweled daggers, as delicate as dragonflies. He spun and slashed with them like a berserker.

Torrents just stood back and launched lightning bolts and hurricane winds. Jack could deflect the bolts and slice through the winds with the Sword of Cortés—but only if he wasn't using it to ward off blows from Stone-Eyed Sam.

Fitzwilliam finally drew his sword, prepared to jump in and help Jack.

Torrents casually waved his hand over his shoulder. A cyclone blew out and picked up the aristocrat. It carried him over to the top of a tree and stranded him in its highest branches.

"Sorry Jack," Fitzwilliam said weakly, clinging desperately.

"It's the thought that counts," Jack called back. His head was spinning from looking back and forth at the two pirates. How was he going to get Stone-Eyed Sam to hold the watch?

He lunged at the mad pirate's chest with the Sword of Cortés.

Stone-Eyed crossed his arms and caught its blade between the two daggers. He yanked, and the Sword of Cortés went flying out of Jack's grasp—and into Sam's.

"Blast!" Jack spat.

Immediately Stone-Eyed Sam pointed the Sword, sending bolts of energy back and forth at Jack and Torrents. Both leaped out of the way.

Then Torrents called forth a tiny cyclone and sent it spinning up Stone-Eyed Sam's right arm. The storm pirate closed his hand into a fist and the cyclone shrunk. It crushed the blade out of Stone-Eyed's hand.

The pirate king howled with rage and pulled out his two daggers again, charging at Torrents.

Jack dove for the Sword, but a dust devil got to it first, carrying it back to Torrents.

Torrents took it, tossing his own sword aside. He immediately started shooting lightning bolts out of his left hand and energy bolts out of his right with the Sword of Cortés.

Jack turned to attack Torrents, to try and get the Sword back.

Then he stopped. The point of this crazy little exercise was to keep Stone-Eyed Sam distracted while handing him the watch outside, under the moon and sun. In the battle for the Sword, he had almost forgotten that!

Now was a perfect time to "hand" the watch to Stone-Eyed, while he was occupied fighting Torrents. Jack pulled the watch out, unsure how to do it.

Then Torrents sent a bolt of lightning at

Stone-Eyed Sam's left hand. It heated the dagger white-hot. The pirate dropped it, screaming.

When Stone-Eyed Sam went to attack Torrents again, Jack darted nimbly in behind him. He swung the watch over his head like a bola.

Fitzwilliam and Tia Dalma both grimaced. It was a *delicate*, powerful, magical time-altering watch, after all.

Jack let it go. The watch flew through the air—and neatly wrapped itself around Stone-Eyed's left wrist and dangled precariously from his hand.

"Let's hope that's close enough," Jack breathed.

The watch began to chime: *Ching*.

Meanwhile, with an unearthly effort, Stone-Eyed sunk his remaining dagger into Torrents's thigh—and then punched straight up into the storm-pirate's face.

Torrents roared, as the blood coming from his broken nose blinded him. Stone-Eyed Sam grabbed him and threw him over his shoulder to the ground.

Ching.

Jack stood nervously aside, wondering if he should help, or attack Torrents, or just stay out of the way.

Torrents bellowed. A small hurricane rose up around the two pirates, sweeping up leaves and debris. They scrabbled in the dirt, partially hidden by the clouds of dust.

Ching.

Stone-Eyed Sam rolled out, clutching the Sword of Cortés. The pocket watch on him flew about—but it was still wrapped around his wrist. Torrents screamed. Lightning flashed. He was losing control of his anger—and his curse.

Ching.

"How many was that?" Jack called out.

"FOUR!" Fitzwilliam shouted.

Stone-Eyed Sam snaked one bony hand around Jack's ankle and pulled. Unprepared, Jack fell forward, hitting the dirt face-first.

Ching.

"I've had enough of your interference!" Stone-Eyed Sam roared. He grinned insanely, each of his crooked teeth glowing in the bloodred light of the Sword. He reached into his shirt and pulled out a curved knife.

"How many bloody weapons do you have on you?" Jack demanded, desperately trying to pull away.

Ching.

A blast of lightning got Stone-Eyed Sam in the back of the head, burning great chunks of his hair off. He shrieked in pain.

Torrents rose. His face was black and blue and swollen.

"Thanks, mate," Jack said cheerfully, extricating himself from the other pirate's grasp.

Torrents responded by shooting another bolt—at Jack.

Ching.

Jack tried to raise his cutlass to block the bolt, but he was still quite winded and it grazed him, shocking him and knocking him down.

Torrents turned back to Stone-Eyed Sam. Hail the size of small cannonballs began to fall from the sky.

Stone-Eyed Sam just grinned and held up the Sword of Cortés. A ray of red energy shot out, evaporating the hail as it fell.

Ching.

"The watch!" Tia Dalma called out.

Jack was too wounded and tired for a witty reply. He put a hand to his side—the last blow must have broken a rib or two. He pulled himself up, using his cutlass as a crutch. How many chimes had the pocket watch played? Eight? Nine?

Ching.

With a howl, Stone-Eyed Sam brought the Sword of Cortés down so its red rays hit Torrents in the eyes. The huge pirate staggered back, clutching his face.

Grinning, Stone-Eyed Sam leaped up with renewed energy. He turned to Jack. His whole body was glowing red now. Even the socket behind his stone eye.

Ching.

The red energy reached over to Jack. He was paralyzed. A heat far worse than the volcano's began to build up on his skin. Jack sank to his knees in pain.

Ching.

Stone-Eyed Sam, with smoke rising from where the lightning had burned him, stood over Jack. With an incoherent scream, he raised the Sword of Cortés over Jack's head.

"JACK!" Fitzwilliam cried.

Jack looked up as the cursed sword came down toward his head. There was nothing he could do. He was too weak to roll aside. It didn't matter, anyway. The watch was about to chime a twelfth time, and when it did, Jack would vanish as history was erased from underneath him.

Ching!

Just before the clock struck twelve, a hand whipped out and yanked the watch off of Stone-Eyed's wrist.

It was Tia Dalma!

Immediately, Stone-Eyed Sam started to fade. His skin turned gray and began to peel back from his flesh. The rest of him then burned away, until all that was left was a single plume of white smoke. The Sword vanished, too, to Jack's disappointment.

Torrents remained, but he had been knocked out cold by the blast of power from the Sword of Cortés.

"Good thing I hadn't handed *him* the watch," Jack muttered, dusting himself off.

A great shifting of light and shadow occurred in the sky above. The "night" sky quickly disappeared, leaving only daylight. The flocks of wheeling Uglybirds vanished. Down on the beach, the Aztec sailors also faded one by one.

"Behold," Tia Dalma pointed at the temple.

In seconds, the stones aged and crumbled, while vines grew up over everything. A thin, bony dust settled. Jack raced back into the throne room. It was just the way he had once

found it: broken and ruined, with no explor-
ers dangling in a cage from the ceiling.

"Whew. History—and my seafaring self—
are saved," Jack groaned in relief, leaning
against a pillar.

The tree Fitzwilliam was in aged and fell
over gracefully. He hopped out, surprised by
his easy release. Tia Dalma reached over and
placed a soft finger on his neck.

Fitzwilliam jumped at the personal
contact.

"My mark has vanished," she explained
with a smile. The crab tattoo she had magi-
cally placed on him was gone.

"I told you when you delivered my pay-
ment you would be unmarked."* She
grinned.

"Now. There is just one thing left to do."

---

* Tia Dalma promised this back in Vol. 7, *City of Gold*.

CHAPTER TEN

"Get me some icy-cold coconut milk, a lift back to the *Barnacle*, and as far away from this island as a man can get in this world," Jack said.

Tia Dalma was deliberately making her way back to the shore. Jack sighed and motioned for Fitzwilliam to follow. Tia Dalma walked to the water's edge and stood defiantly, feet planted.

"Davy Jones!" she called out to the *Flying Dutchman*. She almost sounded like an angry mother calling for a wayward child. Jack and Fitzwilliam looked at each other, confused. And nervous.

"No offense, but I don't know if that's the *best* course of action," Jack said. "We've just spent the better part of the day *getting away* from Captain Jones!"

Tia Dalma just smiled. "*Dutchman!* I *demand* you allow me aboard!"

"Oh, Jones is truly not going to like that," Fitzwilliam said sorrowfully.

Clouds gathered on the horizon. The sea churned and boiled around the *Dutchman*. A wind blew down the beach so hard it blasted sand into Jack's and Fitzwilliam's eyes. When they looked up, there was a skiff bobbing in the waters, apparently waiting for Tia Dalma. It was empty but for a single lantern in the prow. She smiled and stepped delicately in.

"We'll wait here, then," Jack said.

She did not turn back. In moments, the skiff disappeared into the fog.

A half hour later Fitzwilliam and Jack were still waiting for her. The aristocrat stood stiff as a board, hand to his eyes for a better view. Jack sat in the sand, kicking it into little mounds.

Suddenly, the sea boiled again. Like a horrible, ancient sea monster, the *Flying Dutchman* slowly submerged under water. Gray and yellow foam bubbled up from where it had disappeared.

"Good lord! What now?" Fitzwilliam cried out.

Jack frowned. Was she a prisoner of Davy Jones again?

"Fare thee well, Davy Jones," came an amused voice from behind the boys.

Jack jumped up. Fitzwilliam spun around.

There stood Tia Dalma, looking smug. And dry.

"I'll never know how you do these things," Jack observed. "What the blazes did you do to make him go away?"

"We discuss de ways of the winds and de voices of the sea," Tia Dalma said. A look of sorrow passed over her face. "I do believe him seen the error of him ways now. Should he try to return to that time Calypso had forsaken him, she would tear him heart out *for* him, and nothing would be different this day. This trinket is useless now. Its power is gone."

She opened up her hand and dropped the watch into Jack's.

"Hello? It is still *mine*," Fitzwilliam complained. "My pirate-napped sister gave it to me before she disappeared. . . ."

Jack rolled his eyes and tossed the watch

over his shoulder. Fitzwilliam dove to catch it before it landed in the sand.

Jack was about to say something funny, something *really good* to Tia Dalma, when he felt a sudden wave of heat behind him.

Chantico appeared in a blur of flame. She stepped forward, and though the grass was alight with flame, it was not consumed. And then she did something completely unexpected—she *bowed* to Tia Dalma.

"Too much time has passed since we last met," the volcano goddess said in her strange, icy voice.

And then something else unexpected happened: Tia Dalma looked lost. She frowned and clicked her tongue in anguish. "Forgive me. I am . . . only beginning to remember who I am and where I have been."

"You will remember all things in time. And you will be free again. I am sure of it,"

Chantico said with a very—*very*—small smile.

Tia Dalma frowned again, trying hard to remember. But it was no use.

Jack raised his eyebrows. What was all this?

"Probably from spending too much time in the swamps," he decided. "That would drive you right batty. Just like this whole batty conversation. They never make sense when you talk to them one-on-one, soothsayers and goddesses and whatnot. But put them together and abandon hope all ye who enter here!"

"*Captain* Jack Sparrow. Fitzwilliam P. Dalton the *Third*," Chantico said, turning to them. "You have reversed the course of the watch and set the moon and stars back on their normal paths."

"A simple 'thank you' would be enough,"

Jack said. ". . . Unless you have gold. You don't, do you? Have gold, I mean. Do goddesses ever dabble in precious metals?"

Chantico gave him a frosty look. Which was odd, considering the flames dancing around her head.

"Why should you be thanked for correcting what you yourself corrupted?" she demanded.

"I suppose that makes some sort of sense. In a volcano-goddess sort of way," Jack said. Then he gave her a low bow. "Well, I must be on my way. Back to my ship and all. So much to do, so many people to see. Or avoid. Or both. Will you be needin' a lift then, Ms. Dalma?"

There was no answer.

Jack looked up, still bowing.

But no one was there except for Fitzwilliam. The two women were gone.

"I will never get used to the way those types come and go," he said. Then he grinned and began stomping back toward his beloved *Barnacle*.

"So where are we off to now, Jack?" Fitzwilliam asked, slashing at a bit of undergrowth with a flourish of his sword.

"'We?' *I'm* off for more adventure, with real treasure this time. Not volcanoes and Drags and dead sea captains. X marks the spot, mate. That's what it's all about. Or maybe a vacation," he said, suddenly looking thoughtful. "Fiji, maybe? Crystal waters, blue skies, friendly locals . . ."

"I would rather like to see the East," Fitzwilliam said. "The Indies, or even Japan. I have read about some of their temples and feats of engineering. Most remarkable!"

Jack mouthed what the nobleman's son

was saying, rolling his eyes. "This isn't one of those 'schools-on-a-ship,' Fitzy. This is the *Barnacle*. And this is—"

He stopped.

"'This is' *what*, Jack?" Fitzwilliam asked. Traditionally he waited until the *end* of one of Jack's rants before delivering a snotty reply. He didn't want to break form now.

But Jack was stopped dead still. His jaw had dropped open. A look of horror was on his face; one that Fitzwilliam had never seen before. Not even when they came upon monsters, sirens, serpents, port officials, or rotten fish.

He was staring out to sea. There, just beyond the *Barnacle* and gaining fast on her was a rundown pirate ship.

It flew a Jolly Roger that apparently Jack was all too familiar with.

"We've got to get out of here, mate," Jack said, panicking. He took off toward the

Barnacle, almost falling on the sand several times in his hysteria. There was no joking, fast-talking, elaborate explanations, or ridiculous scheming. He just ran for his boat.

Fitzwilliam followed.

Jack didn't say a word the whole time they rowed the tiny skiff out to the *Barnacle*, or when they climbed aboard.

Once on deck, however, Jack let out a scream. He pointed out to sea, speechless for once.

The Royal Navy was on the horizon. In fact, it was what looked like the *whole* Royal Navy—in neat, crowded formation. Coming up fast on the pirate ship. *And* the *Barnacle*.

"Haul anchor," Jack commanded. He reached down and began pulling on the anchor's line for dear life. "I wish we had the *Fleur de la Morte*."*

* Captain Laura Smith's ship, which can disappear when the sails are unfurled, was introduced in Vol 5. *The Age of Bronze*.

Jack rushed over to the sails and unfurled them himself, not even waiting for Fitz-william. He spun the wheel. He tested the wind. He blew into the sails as hard as he could, puffing his cheeks.

But the *Barnacle* was just a little boat, and Jack didn't have the power to command the winds. They only had two hundred feet on the pirate ship now and less than a half league on the Navy . . . it would only be a matter of minutes before they were over-come. Short of a miracle, nothing could stop this from happening.

"Blast and blighters," Jack swore, pacing up and down the deck, running his hands wildly through his hair. "Does anyone else magical owe me a favor?" he thought desper-ately. "The Sea Hag? No, not since that one time I stood her up. . . . The North Wind? What do I do, what do I do?"

Then he felt a sharp point in his back.

He turned around slowly, too stunned to put his hands in the air.

It was Fitzwilliam, and he had his rapier aimed at Jack's middle.

He looked much more relaxed than usual. In fact, his whole countenance had changed.

"We knew you'd lead us to him," he growled in a much deeper voice than he normally used.

"Fitzy," Jack said, honestly confused. "What on earth is going on here?"

But the other boy ignored him, continuing his rant. "'Pretend to be a teenage aristocrat,' they told me. 'Sneak aboard whatever boat they steal,' they said. I told them they were foolish to think you would ever lead us to him, but how wrong I was. You—a petty boy, who was not even a proper pirate."

"Hey, watch what you say about your

captain," Jack said weakly, swallowing hard.

"Now we have both of you," Fitzwilliam continued. "Jack Sparrow *and* the most wanted pirate on the Seven Seas . . . the keeper of the Pirate Code, TEAGUE!"

The boy grinned nastily.

"Prepare to meet your fate, Sparrow. You and your dear daddy—if that rumor be true and he is the devil what spawned you—will both perish at the hands of the Royal Navy of England!"

Don't miss the next volume in the continuing adventures of Jack Sparrow and the crew of the mighty Barnacle!

Sins of the Father

After the last chapter of this volume, there's not much more to say, is there? Find out exactly who Fitzwiliam is working for, learn more about Teague, and watch Jack try to escape his worst predicament yet. All this, and you'll meet A man named Joshamee, too. . .